A Beta's Haven

A Redwood Pack Novella

By
CARRIE ANN RYAN

A Beta's Haven

Being the Beta of the Redwood Pack isn't an easy task, but Jasper has never complained. He's spent his entire adult life dropping everything so he can take care of others. Now he's a father, a husband...and tired. His mate, Willow, knows Jasper won't let others know that he might need a break, even for a weekend, so that's where she comes in.

Once Jasper lets go and allows his mate to call the shots, this Beta might just be in for the ride of a lifetime.

Author's Note: This is a novella set between books 6 and 7 to give you a taste of Jasper and Willow. It is best that you have already immersed yourselves in the Redwood Pack world, however even new readers will enjoy a glimpse of one of the Redwood's favorite couples.

Dedication

Charity H. Thank you for taking over so much of my world, my life, and my sanity.

Acknowledgements

I love writing these little novellas that look into our mates and Redwood families after the HEA. Jasper and Willow's book *A Taste for a Mate* was the first full length book I had ever written and I have learned so much through them and since then. Thank you Devin, Lia, Charity, Michele, and Saya for helping me along the way.

Thank you Scott for an amazing cover and for your understanding when I say I want one thing and then change my mind two minutes later. I can't help it. I'm special like that.

Thank you readers for taking this journey with me. Each time you read my book I swear a

Redwood Pack member finds their mate. *grins*

Redwood Pack Characters

    With an ever growing list of characters in each book, I know that it might seem like there are too many to remember. Well don't worry; here is a list so you don't forget. Not all are seen in this exact book, but here are the ones you've met so far. As the series progresses, the list will as well.

    Happy reading!

Adam Jamenson—Enforcer of the Redwood Pack, third son of the Alpha. Mate to Bay and father to Micah. Story told in *Enforcer's Redemption* and *Forgiveness*.

Anna Jamenson—late mate of Adam.

Bay Jamenson—new member of the Redwood Pack. Mate to Adam and mother to Micah. Story told in *Enforcer's Redemption* and *Forgiveness*.

Beth—member of the Redwood Pack. Aunt to Emily.

Brie Jamenson—daughter of Jasper and Willow.

Cailin Jamenson—Only daughter of Edward and Pat.

Camille—deceased former member of the Redwood Pack.

Caym—demon from Hell summoned by the Centrals. Lover of Corbin.

Charlotte Jamenson—half-sister of Ellie's. Will be raised as a daughter by Ellie and Maddox.

Conner Jamenson—son of Josh, Reed and Hannah. Twin to Kaylee.

Corbin Reyes—new Alpha of the Central Pack. Lover of Caym.

Cyrus Ferns—deceased former unit teammate of Josh's.

Donald—member of the Redwood Pack.

Edward Jamenson—Alpha of the Redwood Pack. Mate to Pat.

Father to Kade, Jasper, Adam, Reed, Maddox, North and Cailin.

Ellie Jamenson—Daughter of the former Alpha of the Central Pack. Mate to Maddox and mother to Charlotte. Story told in *Shattered Emotions*.

Emily—young member of the Redwood Pack. Orphan and niece of Beth.

Emeline—elder of the Redwood Pack. Lost her mate in the first war with the Centrals.

Finn Jamenson—son of Kade and Melanie. Future Heir and Alpha of the Redwood Pack.

Franklin—deceased former member of the Redwood Pack. Camille's lover.

Gina Jamenson—newly adopted daughter of Kade and Melanie. Her birth parents, Larissa and Neil were killed during an attack.

Hannah—Healer of the Redwood Pack. Mate to Josh and Reed. Mother of Conner and Kaylee. Story told in *Trinity Bound* and *Blurred Expectations*.

Hector Reyes—deceased former Alpha of the Central Pack. Father to Corbin, Ellie, Charlotte and Ellie's twin.

Henry—Redwood Pack member and store owner for 60 years.

Isaac—deceased member of the Central Pack.

Jason—member of the Redwood Pack and one of the Alpha's enforcers.

Jasper—Beta of the Redwood Pack. Mate to Willow and father of Brie. Story told in *A Taste for a Mate* and *A Beta's Haven*.

Jim—hot dog vendor and one of Josh's former friends.

Joseph Brentwood—deceased former Alpha of the Talon Pack.

Josh Jamenson—former human Navy Seal. A Finder and

partial demon. Mated to Reed and Hannah. Father to Conner and Kaylee. Story told in *Trinity Bound* and *Blurred Expectations*.

Kade Jamenson—Heir and future Alpha of the Redwood Pack. Mate to Melanie. Father to Finn, Gina, and Mark. Story told in *An Alpha's Path* and *A Night Away*.

Kaylee Jamenson—daughter of Josh, Reed and Hannah. Twin to Conner.

Larissa—deceased member of the Redwood Pack. Witch and friend to Melanie. Mate to Neil and mother of Gina and Mark.

Lexi Jamenson—former Talon Pack member and new Redwood Pack member. Mother to Parker and sister to Logan. Mate to North. Story told in *Hidden Destiny*.

Logan Anderson—former Talon Pack member and new Redwood Pack member. Uncle to Parker and brother to Lexi.

Maddox Jamenson—Omega of the Redwood Pack. Mate to Ellie and father to Charlotte. Story told in *Shattered Emotions*.

Mark Jamenson—newly adopted son of Kade and Melanie.

Her birth parents, Larissa and Neil were killed during an attack.

Melanie Jamenson—former human chemist and mate to Kade. Mother to Finn, Gina and Mark. Story told in *An Alpha's Path* and *A Night Away*.

Meryl—Redwood Pack Elder.

Micah Jamenson—son of Adam and Bay.

Mrs. Carnoski—elderly customer of Josh's when he was human.

Neil—deceased member of the Redwood Pack. Mate to Larissa and father of Gina and Mark.

Noah—member of the Redwood Pack and former lover of Cailin's.

North Jamenson—doctor in the Redwood Pack, son of the Alpha. Mate to Lexi. Story told in *Hidden Destiny*.

Parker Jamenson—new member of the Redwood Pack and son of Lexi's.

Patricia (Pat) Jamenson—mate of the Alpha, Alpha female, and mother to Kade, Jasper, Adam, Reed, Maddox, North, and Cailin.

Patrick—disgruntled member of The Redwood Pack.

Reed Jamenson—artist and son of the Alpha of the Redwood Pack. Mate to Josh and Hannah. Story told in *Trinity Bound* and *Blurred Expectations*.

Reggie—deceased former member of the Central Pack.

Samuel—deceased former member of the Central Pack.

Willow Jamenson—former human baker and now mate to Jasper. Mother to Brie. Story told in *A Taste for a Mate* and *A Beta's Haven*.

CHAPTER ONE

The warm, willing woman in his arms moaned, and Jasper Jamenson pulled her closer, loving the way she arched into him. She was soft, perfect. His. The delicate skin under his hands was familiar, and yet, with each touch, it was like finding something new, something precious, created only for him. His eyes were closed, but he knew he wasn't dreaming, at least he hoped he wasn't. He'd hate to have that happen. Again.

His mate, the love of his life, and his partner, Willow, wiggled her ass against his cock, and he moaned.

Loudly.

"Not so loud, Jasper, you'll wake Brie," Willow whispered, her voice heavy with sleep, gradually filling with need. He felt her body shaking—from holding back laughter or a moan of her own, he wasn't sure. Well, he'd just have to make sure it was the latter. There would be no laughter from his mate while he had his cock pressed against her and when they were both ready to fuck, make love, connect...any of those words that would make them breathe heavy.

He nipped at her neck, and she tilted for him, giving him better access. He licked and sucked at her skin, the salty taste of her body from sleep mixed with the cinnamon that always danced on his tongue when he touched his mouth to her. He'd keep his moans down and try to be quiet, but only because he knew his daughter in the room next to theirs had hearing worthy of any wolf.

"You're the loud one, darling," he teased as he let his hand move to her breast. He plucked at her nipples, loving their reaction to him, pebbling in his palm as he cupped her breasts. He molded them in his hands, taking in their heavy weight. He trailed his hand from between her breasts down over her belly and below the shorts she wore, to the trimmed hair between her legs. He'd never tire of how soft his mate was. Oh, she might not have the full curves of other women, but she was perfect for him.

Willow spread for him, and he circled her clit, his cock hardening even more at the way she plumped for him with just one easy stroke. He'd make her come on his hand, and then, while she was still cascading down from her high, he'd slide his cock into her heat and pump into her until she came again, and he'd come with her.

Yes, that was a good morning he could live with.

He trailed one finger lower and froze as the door creaked open.

"Daddy! It's breakfast time!" Brie squealed.

Jasper heard her little feet tap against the floor as she ran to his side of the bed. He quickly removed his hand from his wife's pants and rolled to his other side so he could stop Brie from jumping into their bed. With just one look, she came to a stop, sliding a bit before regaining her footing. Jasper had his arm out to catch her, but he wasn't needed.

This time.

"Morning, my baby girl," he said, a smile on his face, even though he hadn't gotten to finish what he'd started with his wife. Again. "What did we say about doors in this house, honey?"

She scrunched up her little face. Her brown hair tumbled in a mess around her head as if she hadn't brushed it in weeks, though he knew Willow had put a braid in it before bed. Brie tended to sleep as wildly as she was when awake. Her braid *never* stayed in place.

His perfect little princess wanted to roughhouse with the boys, and Jasper was fine with it. Sure, she might carry a little more dirt than Willow would like, but at least, this way, Brie would learn to fight off the boys when they came knocking at his perfect little princess's door.

Oh, and when they did, Jasper would be ready.

With his claws.

"Uh, don't open it?"

Jasper rolled his eyes then sat up so he could tickle the little monster beside the bed when she moved closer. She giggled, the high-pitched sound grating on his nerves since he'd just woken up, but at least he knew his daughter was happy. He let her go, and she skipped to the door then looked back.

"Is Mommy making breakfast?" his little girl asked, her eyes dancing.

Willow let out a laugh beside him. He sensed her disappointment that they hadn't finished what they'd started, but mixed with that was her amusement of their daughter, so he reached out and squeezed her hand.

"Yes, Brie dear. Or your daddy can make you cereal if you want."

He looked over at his wife and said, tongue in cheek, "Cereal? That's the best I can do? Is that a comment on my cooking, oh-mate-of-mine?"

Willow blinked up at him with those big hazel eyes he loved, the innocence act so not working.

"I have no idea what you mean, love."

Jasper growled, though he couldn't help the corners of his mouth lifting up. "I didn't poison myself with my own cooking before I met you. I won't poison our daughter."

Willow raised a brow, sitting up to fold her arms under her breasts. "If you could find a way to poison anyone pouring a bowl of cereal, you'd be an extra special Beta, wouldn't you?"

Brie giggled then shifted from side to side. Jasper narrowed his eyes. "Did you use your potty this morning?"

"Maybe," was her reply. She scrunched her face, and he held back a curse.

With the rush of a man who was still learning the steps to this whole father-thing, he picked her up, ran her to her training potty, and let her get to work. She wiggled and smiled as she went about her business, and Jasper just leaned against the sink, wondering how the hell he'd ended up here—a place he loved but was drastically different.

He'd been a bachelor for almost a hundred years, the Beta to the Redwood pack, a Jamenson of royal werewolf blood. Now he was a husband, a mate, a father...and the Beta of a Pack who was being attacked on an almost daily basis from the Centrals—a Pack now run by a demon from hell rather than a wolf with a bent on ruling the world.

Yes. Things sure seemed to change in the blink of an eye.

And not all for the best.

He wouldn't change who he was and who he'd become for anything in the world. He loved it all. He'd been there when his baby girl was born, even though Willow had kicked him out of the room a few times. He hadn't been able to help it. He and his wolf had wanted to scream at his brother North for taking too long and letting his mate endure so much pain. He'd been there when his baby girl took her first steps, though he'd missed her first words because he'd been out on a call to fulfill his Beta responsibilities.

He'd been able to watch his wife and mate grow and find a rhythm with her wolf, even though the way she'd turned into one of his kind had been brutal and unyielding. He'd been able to watch his brothers fall in love, bond with their mates, and create the next generation of Jamensons.

Through all of that, he'd accepted his responsibility as the Beta, the one wolf who was bonded to the rest of the Pack in such a way that he knew what they needed, sometimes before they did. It was his job to ensure the needs of the Pack were taken care of so the others around him could function and move forward.

He loved his role in the Pack—even if he was so tired some nights the effort it took to breathe was almost too much.

With the Pack on the defense most days with battles and the threat of war, the health—emotional, physical, and functional—of their members needed to remain high, even if it wasn't necessarily Jasper's job to ensure it. Both he and his wolf knew when a Pack member needed something, such as time off or to focus on a new project, but that didn't mean Jasper had to hold their hand to make it happen.

He did it because he wanted to.

Maddox, his twin brother, was the Omega, so he helped with emotional health of the Pack, much like Hannah, his sister-in-law, the Healer, helped with their physical health.

Jasper was the jack of all trades, doing what the moon goddess needed, even if he didn't have a clear daily job these days.

Between war meetings with the
family, actual battles with the
Centrals, and his duties as Beta,
he didn't spend as much time
with Willow and Brie as he
wanted to, and that hurt above all
else. He could deal with the lack
of sleep and barely scraping by
his responsibilities, but he was
missing so much with his family,
and in that, he knew something
had to change.

He just had no idea what.

If only the Beta could have an
assistant or something.

"Daddy, I'm done."

Jasper blinked and looked
down at his little girl, who smiled
up at him. He helped her wash
her hands, took care of her
training potty, washed his own
hands twice more, and then
carried Brie out of the bathroom
upside down. He could have held
her correctly, but he loved the
way she squealed. He dodged a

stray kick to the chin and kept moving.

As he moved, he caught a newer scent coming from his baby girl, one that had more to do with the magic within her ready to burst free than anything she might have rolled in. Knowing Brie, she could have rolled in just about anything.

His wolf nudged up against him, and he smiled. Yes, his little girl would be doing her shift soon. His own wolf could tell. All werewolves were born human, and usually, between the ages of two and three, they made their first shift into wolf pups. At that age, they had a little more control over their bodies to make the change, though all pups were a little rambunctious.

"Down, Daddy, down!" Brie giggled, the high-pitched sound not as grating now that he was awake, but damn, he needed coffee.

He set her down on her feet, and she scrambled to her chair in the dining room. Jasper followed his nose to the scent of fresh coffee then leaned against the archway so he could watch Willow in her element. No, he wasn't being a chauvinistic ass. His Willow loved cooking and was freaking amazing at it. He still remembered the taste of the first omelet she'd made for him in this house and how he'd wanted to kneel at her feet and ask her to stay forever.

Okay, he might have done that anyway because his love and need for her wasn't only for her omelets.

He licked his lips at the scent of the cinnamon from the rolls in the air blending with the sugar and cinnamon from his mate's skin. He and his wolf loved the fact that his mate carried the scent of her famous cinnamon rolls on her skin.

Yep, she was totally perfect for him.

He came up from behind her and pulled her close. She laid her head back and sighed. "I'm almost done, then the rolls will have to bake for twenty minutes. I know Brie is hungry now, but I was in the mood for something extra sweet."

He nibbled at her neck and hummed against her. "Me too, love."

Willow laughed and wiggled away, the motion only making his cock stand more at attention. "Shoo. Go get Brie her yogurt so she at least has something nutritious. She can have half a roll when they're done."

He did as he was told and sat next to his daughter as she ate, laughing and telling him a story about her cousin Finn and how he'd turned into his wolf then tried to climb on a picnic table but had forgotten he had four paws instead of two feet.

He leaned back, sipping on his coffee, trying to ignore the long list of items he needed to get through and just listened to his daughter ramble. When she finished her story and ate more of her yogurt, she danced in her seat, unable to keep still for even a moment.

Jasper ran a hand through his hair, noticing it was again reaching his shoulders. His mother would scold him in that sweet way of hers, but Willow seemed to like it. Still, he needed to start taking better care of himself.

"Hey, Willow, what do you say the three of us go for a picnic or something today?"

Willow came out of the kitchen to the dining room, a frown on her face as she dried her hands. "Don't you have to go to Isaiah's house today then Ms. Clerk's? They need your help with fixing something or other. After that, you have that meeting with Adam about patrols. You have to make sure that people are getting their shifts worked out, so they have a breather like they should, even though I think Adam knows that already."

Jasper shook his head and stood up so he could bring her closer. "I think everyone can handle a day without me. Right?" Before the war, before he'd had his family, he'd been able to do just that. Now, though, things were different.

Willow smiled, her eyes bright. "I'd love it if you could do that. I have people coming into the bakery today to work. I was planning on taking the day off to play with Brie anyway. We'd love it if you could come with us."

He grinned, his body relaxing for the first time in too long. He brought his lips to hers and sank against his mate.

His cell phone rang on the counter, and he cursed. "Let's hope that's something I can ignore."

Willow gave a sad smile, patted his cheek, and then shook her head. "I know you love your job as Beta, Jasper. No, that's not right... It's not a job; it's your calling, your duty. Do what you need to. Brie and I will be here. I promise."

He kissed her forehead then picked up his cell. Of course it wasn't something he could ignore, as it was one of the newly widowed witches in the Pack, Calista, who'd lost her husband during one of the Centrals' attacks. Emotionally, she was a wreck, but she was maintaining with Maddox's help. Jasper also had a duty to her, to be there to make sure she had all she needed to raise her kids, live her life, and try to find a way to move on.

After dressing for the day, and following a regretful kiss goodbye to his girls, he made his way to Calista's. She was in a rare position in that she didn't have any family within the den to help with things like a leaky pipe in her basement—the current job Jasper had to help with. Yes, his actual job in the human world, when he could get to it, was a contractor, but he barely remembered that world these days. Calista, however, didn't have a job in the human realm. She'd been a stay-at-home wife to her mate and mom to her six children, something she loved.

Mateo, her late husband, had been one of the Alpha's enforcers, a bodyguard to the Alpha, and had died protecting the Pack on patrol. Now Calista was alone, with no family except for Mateo's great aunt who, at four hundred and twelve, was long past the age of wanting to help raise kids. She did it though. Calista wasn't alone and was a strong enough woman that her kids were in a better place than they would have been if she hadn't had such a steely backbone.

The woman couldn't fix a leaky pipe though—something that pissed her off.

"I don't understand it, Jasper," she said as she soothed her four-year-old and brushed her six-year-old's hair at the same time. "If it was just a normal leak, I could fix it, but this? This looks big."

Well, she wasn't wrong. The woman's basement currently resembled a small lake. Since Calista wasn't a wolf and didn't have those extra senses, she hadn't been able to hear the room filling with water. She'd caught it before it had gotten any worse only because one of her kids had noticed it.

"You could call it that," Jasper answered easily. "I'm going to have to call Kade or someone else in to help me fix it."

Calista sighed but nodded. "Is there something special I need to know about for cleanup?"

"Yeah, but I'll bring people over to help. You've got enough on your plate to worry about mold."

"Oh goddess. Mold?" Her voice rose to a squeak, and Jasper winced.

"We'll take care of it. Don't you worry." He ran a hand over one of the little girls' hair, missing his own Brie.

"I don't know what I'd do without you, Jasper. I don't know what the Pack would do you without you. You're a great Beta."

Jasper gave a tight smile and got to work. Yes, he might have been a great Beta, but he was a fucking tired one. He'd wanted to spend time with his girls, and now he was knee-deep in murky water.

Oh, the joys of duty and fate.

He loved his job, he really did. He just wanted to go back to a time when he had something else...something that was just about him.

Something gurgled behind him, and he turned, only to find himself drenched and dripping with sewage.

Fuck it.

He looked down at what he hoped was mud on his shirt.

He needed a vacation.

Or at least a towel.

Jasper let out a breath then bent to pick up his tool box from the steps. Seeing how he was mired in his own head and not paying attention like he should have been, he didn't see the rusty pipe sticking out of the wall.

His head slammed into it, and he saw stars, swallowing back bile as he fell to his knees, the water now up to his chest.

He blinked a couple times, and then, just as the darkness slid over him, he heard shouts and his name.

At least he wouldn't drown alone. He definitely needed a break.

CHAPTER TWO

The scent of cinnamon hung in the air and danced along her taste buds as Willow Jamenson snuck a bite of one of her buns after she'd iced it and the other forty in her bakery. The heat scorched the roof of her mouth, but she didn't care. The sugar and sweet hit the spot, and she groaned. She hadn't been this hungry and craving cinnamon like her mate tended to since she'd been pregnant with Brie. She was a hundred percent sure she wasn't pregnant right then thanks to a home test and talking with Hannah, the Pack Healer, who was also her sister-in-law, so she was sure the craving had to come from stress.

Stress resulting from what her mate and love was going through at the moment. It had been four days since she'd gotten the frantic call from Calista saying that Willow had to come over and help Jasper because he'd knocked himself in the head, fallen over, and almost drowned. Luckily Kade had just shown up to help him out and had managed to pull Jasper out of the water before he went under fully, but it had been a close one.

The Beta of the Redwood Pack had almost drowned in a

leaky basement, all because of a rusty pipe.

Gods, Willow couldn't even think it. She shuddered, her skin going clammy as she tried to push away the memory of how pale he'd looked when she'd arrived at the house. She'd called Cailin on the way and met her outside so she could leave Brie with her. There was no hiding her tension and fear from her little girl, but at least she hadn't had to bring her inside, which had kept her from seeing her daddy looking so...small...defeated.

Jasper had always been bigger than life to her. He'd come into her bakery when she'd lived outside the den, unaware that the monsters that lived in closets were actually real, and had ordered a cinnamon roll and coffee. He'd known who she was to him through his wolf and the man. He'd wanted her to be his mate for no other reason than he loved who she was. It was icing on the cake that his wolf agreed. But he'd been taking his time, courting in a way she hadn't understood until it had almost been too late.

Now they were fully mated, both wolves, and parents.

Yet her Jasper was floundering because the man didn't know how to say no.

He'd hit his head on a damn rusty pipe—something he never would have done with a clear head—and had almost died. She still couldn't believe it.

She hated feeling as though she was useless to help those she loved. She'd spent her entire human life not being able to do what she needed to do, so she refused to have her life as a wolf follow the same path.

However, this wasn't a job just for her. The role as Beta was handed down from the moon goddess herself and couldn't be refused. That didn't mean, though, that Willow would stand back and watch her husband and mate drain himself to the point that he couldn't function. He wasn't happy, and they both knew it.

Things were going to have to change, but getting there wasn't going to be easy.

The bell on top of the door rang, and she smiled, knowing who stood on the other side by their scents. She turned as a little ball of brown hair and spastic energy ran at her, jumping before Willow had even turned around fully.

Brie fell into her arms easily and screamed "Momma!" at the top of her lungs, the happiness and excitement of her day all but radiating off of her.

Willow blinked at the ringing in her ears then put her forehead to her daughter's. "What did we say about screaming indoors?" There was no way they'd be able to contain her little girl's excitement about life in general twenty-four hours a day, so they'd said she could yell and laugh all she wanted outdoors where it wouldn't be as hard on a wolf's hearing.

At least that was the idea.

Brie was one loud, exuberant little girl.

"Sorry," her little girl whispered. "I just missed you." Brie laid a sloppy kiss on her cheek, and Willow knew she was a goner for her daughter's kisses and love. The Jamensons might joke that Jasper was wrapped around Brie's little finger, but Willow was right there with her mate.

"I missed you too, darling," Willow whispered back then moved so she could see the others who had come in with Brie.

Maddox wasn't smiling, but she could see the laughter in his eyes. As the Omega, he didn't smile often, considering he wore the weight of the Pack's emotions on his shoulders, but since he'd mated with Ellie, he'd been much better about letting a little glimpse of what he was thinking and feeling shine through. He had his daughter, Charlotte, by his side, her face dimpled in a smile.

It was good to see her smile considering where she'd spent the first five years of her life. The Centrals had raised her to five, and thank God, she'd been left untainted.

Cailin stood beside Maddox, an odd expression on her face, almost one of intense longing, but she'd schooled her features back to her normal air of Aunt Cailin.

"The little munchkins wanted cookies, and who are we to deprive them of sugar?"

Maddox let out a little growl then picked up Charlotte so he could blow a raspberry on her stomach. The action brought out laughter from not only Charlotte, but Willow as well.

He set Charlotte down on her feet and glared at his sister. "Thank you for giving them sugar, considering you're not going home with any of them to deal with the results before the crash."

Again that expression of longing washed over her face, and Maddox let out a curse. Willow stayed back, knowing that whatever Cailin was feeling at the moment was between Maddox and her. Maddox only knew it because of his powers, and despite how close the Jamensons were, some things weren't meant to be shared.

"Come on, Charlotte, let's pick out what kind of cookie you'd like. We have the thick frosting sugar ones I know you've had before." Charlotte, as usual, quietly walked to Willow's side and held her hand.

Willow got both girls their cookies and corralled them in the corner play area that Jasper and Kade had designed for the numerous Pack children. When she was done, she sat down at a nearby table with Cailin and Maddox.

"So, why did you want Maddox and me here specifically?" Cailin asked, getting right to the point. Willow loved that about her sister-in-law.

"I need help." She took a deep breath. "No, *we* need help."

Maddox tilted his head, displaying that odd look he got on his face when he was reading another's emotions. "This is about Jasper's accident."

"I can't believe big brother did that." Cailin ran a hand through her hair, her eyes wide.

Willow shook her head hard. "He did that because he's exhausted and being pulled in a million directions." She looked around her empty bakery, glad that it was the downtime of the day so they had privacy. "When we weren't at war and everyone could come and go from the den in peace, it was different. He didn't have to do *everything* for so many people. As more and more people get hurt, or just feel a need for comfort, to be closer to the powers that hold the Pack together, Jasper's spreading himself too thin. I don't know how to help my mate, and it's killing me."

Maddox gripped her hand, and she immediately felt relief. He was siphoning her fear and anger into himself, and while that was great, she *needed* those emotions to get the next part of her plan in place.

She pulled away, giving him a small smile. "Thanks for that, but what I really need is for some way to share Jasper's duties with another person or find a way for him to have a break. I know he'll be angry that I'm going behind his back on this, but I don't know what else to do. He's so stubborn when it comes to being the Beta. I get it. It's his role and duty, and he loves it. I love that he loves it. I love that he puts his all into the Pack, but he's killing himself over things that only matter day-to-day, but not in the grand scheme of things. There's got to be a way to help him."

Maddox tilted his head and studied her. Though she'd known the wolf, her brother-in-law, since she'd become part of the Redwoods, the way he stared still unnerved her. The man could sense every emotion she had, though she knew he tried to dampen his abilities from his family to give everyone a semblance of privacy.

As wolves, though, there wasn't much of that, not with their heightened senses, bonds, and, as with the Jamensons, special connections through their roles and powers.

"You're good for my brother," he finally said.

Even though Willow wanted to roll her eyes at the statement, she still blushed. She'd grown up without family and sometimes forgot what it felt like to be with people who cared about each other beyond measure.

"He's good for me," she replied then stole a peek at Charlotte and Brie, who were playing with blocks. Or, rather, Brie was playing, trying to build something while Charlotte built a little wall around them both, protecting them with her fortress.

"What do you need from us?" Cailin asked, straight to the point as usual.

"I'm not sure. I do need your help, but I don't know exactly what you can and cannot do when it comes to the moon goddess's powers."

Maddox nodded. "We can't remove or change his powers. That's not something within our grasp, nor is it something that any of us—including Jasper— would want to do."

Willow shook her head. "No, I wouldn't want that. Jasper loves his duties and knows it's his calling. I know it is as well. We just need a breather. I know Kade and Mel found a way to do that before. Wow, was it over a year ago already? It seems like just yesterday, yet also like so long ago."

Maddox grinned, the scar on his face tugging a bit. "I remember that vividly, considering I had to babysit Finn." He looked over at Charlotte. "Though I never had to go through Charlotte's diaper phase, I did help with Finn's." He shot a look at Cailin. "And yours too." His sister punched him in the arm, hard from the way the Omega winced. "I suppose I will have to go through that phase again when Ellie and I have more children."

Willow sighed. She wanted more children as well. She and Jasper had always planned on having another child close to Brie's age. Though werewolves lived extremely long lives, most of them tried to have their children within short timeframes. That way their children could grow up as siblings to avoid a situation like Cailin's. Given the age differences between her and her brothers, she had grown up surrounded by males who were almost like older uncles, although Edward and Pat had made it work.

Now with the war, the stresses of his position, and the fact that she never had time to make love with her mate, no matter how hard they tried, she didn't see another baby on the way any time soon. Brie was enough to handle as it was.

However, discussion of babies was not on their agenda, even if in a roundabout way it was on the same general subject.

She and Jasper wanted more children in the future and in order to do that, they needed time to breathe...together.

"I ask again, what can we do? Is there a way to relieve him of some of his duties? I don't even think taking a weekend off would do it. He'd just get stressed all over again, and we'd end up in this situation within days. He almost drowned—literally— because he couldn't handle it all. I do not want to lose my husband. Not for the Pack and not because of another Pack."

The latter was a danger they all feared.

She prayed for a solution to the former.

Without living the life they desired, the war would be futile.

Cailin tilted her head and narrowed her eyes, that look telling Willow the woman was up to something. Her striking green

eyes were even brighter than any
of the Jamenson men. Though
the men had varying shades of
hair that ranged from sandy to
back as coal, Cailin's was in a
league of its own, the blue-black
seeming to shine in any lighting.

"What if I helped?" she finally
asked, and Willow felt that knot
in her stomach relax somewhat.

"How?" she asked. She
needed plans. She wasn't as
obsessive about lists as her sister-
in-law Melanie, but she needed
concrete plans if she was going to
find a way to help Jasper.

"I'm not connected to the
Pack like he is, but I can help
anyway."

Cailin shrugged, but Willow
could tell from the way she tried
to blink it away, that the lack of a
special bond bothered Caitlin,
even if she tried to hide it. One
day, if Willow was ever able to
breathe normally again, she'd talk

with her sister-in-law about it. Right now, though, she needed to think about her mate.

"I know you can, Cailin," Willow said. "I'm sorry I sounded snippy just then with asking how, but I need to know. I need to go back to him with a plan, or he'll just tell me he has everything under control. We all know he doesn't. At least not right now."

"No, that's okay. What I can do, though, is take some of his responsibilities. He might *need* to care for the Pack, but he doesn't need to do every little thing himself. We can force the Pack to start calling me or someone else if they need things. I know Jasper also knows when Pack members need help before even they know it, so I can't help there, but I can help with the others. He doesn't and *shouldn't* have to do everything on his own. So I'll help. I need something to do anyway because, as much as I love babysitting my nieces and nephews, I need a purpose that's more than that. I need a goal and plan just for me." She gave a small smile. "And then, when I have one, I can help my family and Pack out at the same time. It's a win-win."

Willow sucked in a shaky breath then launched herself around the table, wrapping her arms around Cailin. "Oh my God, thank you so much."

Cailin hugged her back. Hard. The woman might look standoffish to others sometimes, but she loved to hug just like the rest of the Jamensons. She also did it with all of her heart.

"We'll take care of your mate, Willow."

Tears slid down Willow's cheeks, and she pulled away, wiping them quickly before Brie noticed from over in the little play area. The last thing she wanted was her little girl to be worried over her momma's feelings.

She sniffed once then smiled. "Okay then. So you'll help. Good."

"I'll help her as well," Maddox put in.

Willow shook her head. "No, you have your own powers and responsibilities. I don't want to overwork you."

Maddox just smiled. "Yes, I do, but for the next week, I will help her with some of the needs that I can tell from her emotions. All of our powers are tied together in certain ways that allow the Pack to function. This will give you time to steal Jasper away for a little while and actually enjoy your mate. All of our matings are new, and because of the war, we haven't been able to relish them like we should have."

"I'm sure Mom and Dad would love to have Brie for that

time too. Yes, they're busy like the rest of us, but they love grandbabies."

Willow closed her eyes, the warmth and love of her family filling her and making her want to weep again. She hated crying, and yet she seemed to do it at the drop of a hat when she was stressed.

"Go home with Brie and see your mate," Cailin said. "Let me and Maddox figure out what I'll need to do. I'll even talk with Dad about watching Brie and what our plans are. That way he's in the loop."

Since Edward was the Alpha, it only made sense that he would need to be in the know with any changes or Pack matters. Willow was glad Cailin and Maddox would be helping, but she also didn't want to put everything on their shoulders.

"I don't want you to have to do everything."

Cailin shook her head. "We aren't. We're working as a family to make sure one of our own is happy. Go home to your mate and breathe again. When we have the planning finished, you can kidnap him and make it worth his while." She wiggled her eyebrows, and Willow snorted at the pained look on Maddox's face.

"Don't do that again. For the love of God, stop talking about things like that when it has to do with my brothers. Which, by the way, dear sister, are your brothers too."

Cailin rolled her eyes. "Yeah, but I don't think about that. I was thinking about Willow. Gah."

Willow just shook her head and left the two of them bickering with one last hug. After saying goodbye to her employees who had entered the building a few moments before, she picked up Brie, said goodbye to Charlotte, and walked out of the bakery. She was off shift, and because it was a small den-run place, she knew it would be in good hands when she left.

Since it was a nice walk to her home, she'd decided not to drive that morning. Usually when she had Brie, she would drive just so her little one didn't get cranky. However, today, Brie just laid her head on Willow's shoulder and mumbled sweetly on their journey.

When she walked into the front room, she almost swallowed her tongue.

Jasper stood shirtless, wearing his jeans, tool belt, and boots.

Oh. My.

He turned to her, his long hair tied back with a leather strap. "Hey, there's my girls. I'm fixing something on our deck then I thought we'd head to Adam and Bay's for dinner. That way we don't have to cook." The bright smile on his face didn't hide the shadows on his face, and Willow knew that, even though she was hiding her plans, they were for the best.

She'd do anything to protect her mate.

Even from himself.

CHAPTER THREE

Jasper's head snapped back, and he blinked, the little birds dancing around his face telling him maybe he should sit down. He staggered back, opening his jaw wide and feeling around his mouth with his tongue to make sure he didn't knock lose any teeth.

"Shit, Jasper. I didn't think I'd hit you that hard." Kade

gripped Jasper's elbow and forced him to sit on the nearby rock.

Jasper shook his head then winced. Nope, shouldn't have done that. "I know you didn't mean to. I just didn't move fast enough."

Logan came down to eye level, pushing Kade out of the way. Considering neither Kade nor Logan was a doctor, it didn't really matter which one looked at him, but whatever. Jasper just needed a nap.

"You're really sucking at this fighting stuff, Beta," Logan grunted. "I thought you were the mighty Jamenson and could fight like no other."

Jasper flipped the man off then leaned against the tree trunk that stood behind the large rock he sat on. He still wasn't quite sure how he felt about the other wolf. The man was a good fighter and had proven over and over again that his loyalties ran to the Redwoods. He also took care of his sister, Lexi, and nephew, Parker, better than anyone had before, though now that North was mated to Lexi, Logan was backing off a bit to let the new family gain their balance.

Jasper didn't have a problem with any of that.

The problem was that Logan's wolf happened to be sniffing around Jasper's little sister.

What made it worse was that Cailin was sniffing around him, too.

Cailin might be in her twenties, but she would forever be Jasper's *baby* sister.

His wolf nudged along his skin, wanting to beat the other wolf to a pulp for even daring to look at Cailin, his perfect, precious baby sister. The man, though, had a fucking headache because he'd been too tired and too slow to duck Kade's punch during training.

He'd just have to hurt Logan later.

Jasper rubbed along his jaw, the ache already going away. Kade hadn't hit *too* hard since they were only training, but the punch shouldn't have landed at all.

"You need to go home and get some sleep," Kade said as he rolled his shoulders. "No. First, you need to go make love to your wife, get some food in your system, and then, sleep for a week. You're too fucking tired these days to do anything."

Jasper growled, not liking the fact that his brother was right. "You're just as tired as I am."

Kade shook his head and sat next to him on the rock. Logan paced back and forth in front of them. The other man had a lot more energy than they did, but then again, Logan's wolf was different—not that Jasper knew exactly how yet. That was something else on his list to find out about the other man.

"All of us are tired because of this damn war, but we're not as exhausted as you," Kade said softly. "You need to give yourself a break."

"How? How the hell am I supposed to do that, huh? If I don't continue to do what I'm doing, then I'm letting down the Pack. I won't have them in need because I can't handle my duties. The moon goddess gave me the power to do this, and damn it, I'm going to fucking do it."

"And kill yourself in the process?" Logan asked.

"I'm fine," he lied.

"You're lying," Kade said. "But if you're gonna lie to yourself as well as us, then there isn't anything I can do. I will be by your side if you need me though."

"I'm fine. Really."

"Are you?" Logan asked.

He closed his eyes and ran a hand over his face. "No, no, I'm not fucking okay. I'm pulled in too many directions, and I can't even train with Kade and you without getting my ass kicked. What if I can't protect my family?"

That was his greatest fear. If he was too exhausted to complete his daily tasks, how was he going to protect Willow and Brie if something happened?

His wolf whined, and Jasper knew his wolf had the same feeling sliding through him as well.

"Jasper..." Kade sighed and shook his head.

It seemed not even the Heir knew what to say.

"Can we just drop the subject?" As much as he loved his brother—and tolerated Logan even though he happened to be a little too close to Cailin for Jasper's tastes—he needed to get his mind off his troubles. That was one reason he'd come out to train and fight a bit. He needed to keep his skills up for when they went into hand-to-hand combat with the Centrals, knowing something big was coming.

And they *would* be going hand-to-hand with the Centrals. They'd already done it a few times, and the powder keg was ready to burst.

Kade raised his brows but gave a tight nod. "Okay, I'll drop it for now. Not forever though." He turned to Logan. "So, what would you like to discuss now?"

Logan narrowed his gaze. "Not whatever is on your mind from the look on your face."

Since Jasper had a feeling he and Kade were on the same page when it came to Logan and Cailin, he could see Logan's issue. It wasn't that they didn't *want* a mating. It was that they needed to make sure Logan was good enough for their sister.

And since *no one* was good enough for Cailin, approving a mate choice was a herculean task.

Jasper's head hurt too much to deal with that, so he changed the subject. "How is Melanie?"

Kade snorted and rolled his eyes. "We'll let the other thing drop for now then. As for Mel? She's great. Well, as great as she can be since we're all stressed."

"She's a good Heir's mate," Jasper said. "She'll make a great Alpha female when Dad steps down."

Kade smiled. "Yeah, yeah, she's amazing." He let out a breath. "I feel like I just met her, and yet I know her better than I know myself some days. I can't believe everything that's changed in such a short time."

Jasper nodded, his head finally feeling normal. Thank the goddess he was a werewolf and healed quickly. He felt the same way as Kade when it came to his Willow. He loved the woman with every breath he had and knew his life would have been far darker without her. His wolf nudged at him, wanting to go back to their mate.

The snap of a branch reached his ears, and all three men went on alert. They stood back to back, their fists clenched as they took in the scene. Jasper took a deep breath, inhaling the scents around him then froze, a smile forming on his face.

Cinnamon.

"Willow," he whispered.

She came out from the trees to the small clearing where the men stood and smiled. He noticed a gleam in her eye that meant she was hiding something, but he ignored it for now because she also looked happy. All he wanted was to pick her up and never let her go. It was as if they had just mated.

Gods, he loved her.

"Hey, you, I'm glad you're still here." She came right up to him, stood on her tiptoes, and kissed his chin. He lowered his head and met her lips, having missed her more than he could say.

He tucked a piece of hair behind her ear and studied her face. "What's going on? Is everyone okay?" He felt Kade and Logan still behind him, but the other men were giving them space thankfully.

She just smiled and wrapped her arms around his waist. "Everyone else is fine, but you aren't."

He started. "What?"

"I'm kidnapping you, Jasper Jamenson, and there's nothing you can say or do that will change my mind."

Jasper's wolf nudged along his skin, liking Willow's plan. In fact, Jasper liked the sound of her plan as well.

"What do you mean you're kidnapping me?"

Willow pulled away slightly and looked behind him. "Can I have a moment with my mate?" she asked.

Jasper turned around to see huge grins on Kade's and Logan's faces.

Kade came to Willow's side, pulled her from Jasper's arms, and smacked a loud kiss on her lips. Jasper couldn't help the possessive growl that ripped from his lips.

"Get your hands off my mate and on to your own."

Kade just winked and handed Willow to Logan, who proceeded to kiss her too. Jasper reached out to wring the wolf's neck, but Kade held him back.

"Have fun with your mate, Willow. Don't tire him out too much." With another wink, he and Logan walked away, leaving the two of them in the forest alone.

"I'm going to kill that wolf for touching you."

Willow's mouth twitched. "Which one?"

"Either one. Maybe both." He rubbed his lips against hers than pulled her into a hug. "I don't like their scents on you."

"Then you better find a way to get your scent, and *only* your scent, all over my body."

Jasper's cock hardened, pressing against the zipper of his jeans. "We could arrange that, but, first, tell me what's going on in that head of yours."

"I already told you. I'm kidnapping you."

"You can't just kidnap me, Willow. I have responsibilities. *We* have responsibilities."

She just shook her head. "It's all taken care of. All you have to do is follow me to our SUV and jump in, and then we're driving to one of the cabins on the corner of the den."

"What? When did you plan all of this?" He didn't understand what was happening, though the idea of being alone in a cabin with Willow for any period of time made him want to howl with glee.

His wolf howled a little anyway.

Apparently he was in agreement.

"I've been planning for a little while. I want us to enjoy some time together. Just the two of us. Then, when we get back, we will spend time with Brie. Just the three of us."

He cupped her face and kissed her softly. "You know that's what I want too, baby. I just don't know how you're doing this. We haven't been spending much time together as it is because we *can't*."

"We're taking care of all that. Now come on. I'm kidnapping you, and since you're bigger than me, you'll just have to go along with it so I don't have to knock you out and drag you. You've already had a few too many hits to the head recently."

He blinked down at his mate. "You're joking about that? What's up with you, baby?"

"If I don't joke and make plans to make things better, than

I'd just curl in a ball and cry.
That's not how it works, so we're
going to figure things out. You
can't do it yourself because you're
in the middle of it. If you do focus
on how to fix things rather than
doing it, you'll just end up getting
another concussion because
you're too scattered."

"You are remarkable. I love
you so fucking much. You get
that, right?"

She tilted her head, the
concern in her eyes mixed with
the determination she must have
used to make the plans she'd
made.

"I get that, and I love you just
as much. Now let's get out of
here. We're going to one of the
cabins in the den, but it's really
far out and close to the border."

The words he'd said to Kade
and Logan just before her arrival
floated through his mind. "Is it

safe?" Was he strong enough to protect her if the time came?

"It's as safe as any area of the den these days," she said, not a hint of fear in her tone. It held only resignation.

He hated that he'd brought her into the Pack right at the time of war, and ever since. their world had been fighting around them, and he'd been powerless to stop it. He needed to put that in the back of his mind, though, and focus on what Willow was trying to give him.

Peace.

The walked out of the clearing to where Willow had parked their SUV and got in.

"You drive since you know the area better," she said as she slid into the passenger seat.

"Where are we going?" he asked, starting the engine and inhaling her sweet scent. It seemed to fill the inside of the car quickly.

"The old Clemens cabin."

He knew the place and nodded before heading out.

"What about Brie?" he asked as he gripped Willow's hand. He'd been thinking about Brie since Willow first mentioned her plans, but he hadn't said anything because he knew she'd take care of their daughter first, above all else.

"Your parents have her. She'll be fine, and Mom gets to spoil her."

That sounded about right, and Brie would have a blast.

"What about my Beta duties?" Those he couldn't just forget, and there wasn't another Beta to help him. Hence the situation he was in.

"Cailin is working on them with Maddox. Your family is taking care of you, honey. And when you get back, we will all work to find a way to help you deal with everything. It's not fair that you're doing so much and not asking for help. You know we'd give it to you."

If he hadn't been driving, he'd have fallen to his knees, floored that everyone was planning around him, making sure that *his* well being and wishes were being met.

"Willow—"

"Don't stress. Just get us to the cabin where I can have my way with you. Then we can deal with everything else."

Images of just how she would have her way with him filled his mind, and he groaned before speeding up.

Her laughter made his wolf want to purr like a fucking cat, but he didn't care. In less than twenty minutes, he pulled in front of the cabin and got out. He did a quick check of his surroundings, letting his senses reach out as far as he could.

He didn't sense anything was amiss, so he walked around to the passenger side, where Willow stood, a grin on her face.

"We can unpack the car later," she said, her voice sultry.

"Oh really?" he asked. He knew his eyes had to be glowing gold with arousal because Willow's eyes were as well, and his cock was too fucking hard to even think. Well, he couldn't think, but his cock sure had a mind of its own at the moment.

"Come inside, darling. You need your rest."

"Are you sure I don't need you first?" he asked. Fuck resting. He was finally alone with his mate and wanted her.

Now.

"Oh, I'm sure that can be arranged, but not until after *I*

have *you*." She growled a bit, the sound going straight to his cock.

"You need to relax, my precious Beta, and I'll take good care of you. I'm in charge this time."

He swallowed hard then grinned. He liked this side of Willow, and if she wanted to be in charge and take care of him, then who was he to stand in her way?

"That sounds like a deal, but next time, I get to be in charge. I want to eat that pretty pussy of yours," he said, his voice low and full of promise.

She tilted her head. "Who says I won't tell you to eat me so you can relax?"

He blinked then threw his head back and howled.

Fuck yeah, he loved this woman.

He hurried inside of the small one-room cabin that had a

kitchen and bathroom off to the side.

"Take off your clothes," Willow ordered as she closed the door behind her. She stripped off her shirt and pants, leaving her bare and oh-so-fucking sexy.

"You weren't wearing anything underneath your clothes?" he asked, his voice close to breaking like a freaking teenager's.

"I didn't want to bother. Now strip."

She put an extra wiggle in her step as she walked toward him. He did as he was told and shucked off his clothing. His cock bobbed against his belly, so fucking hard he was afraid if she touched him even once he'd explode.

He grinned as she prowled toward him. She placed her finger in the middle of his chest and pushed. Though he was bigger, and her little push wouldn't have moved him on a normal day, he backed up, allowing her the control she wanted.

Or maybe she was in control anyway and there was no allowing about it.

His mate was fucking perfect.

He backed up a few more steps until the backs of his thighs hit the bed, and he stopped. "Do you want me to sit, lie down, or stand?" he asked, his voice rough. Gods, he wanted to touch her, wanted to feed her, but this was Willow's show, and he was just the willing participant.

She blinked up at him, the need and temptation swirling in those depths mixing with his own, forcing him to swallow, hard. "You just stand right there while I take care of you."

He sucked in a breath as she went to her knees, her nails raking down his hips and thighs.

The slight burn went away in a flash as she licked the crown of his cock.

"Hell, you don't have to do this, Willow." Though he totally wanted her to.

She just rolled her eyes then licked down his cock. "I'm allowed to like blow jobs, you know. I might not be the best at them, but I'm also not the sweet and innocent little lamb who needs to be afraid of your cock."

The laugh burst out of him before he could pull it back. Gods, he loved his Willow. "First, you fucking rock at blow jobs. You know I love them since I usually can't last more than a few minutes with my cock between your lips. Second? You're still sweet and innocent, but wrapped around a vixen that I adore. So I'm just going to stand here like you told me to and keep my mouth shut because I know

70

you're not scared of my cock and I'd rather you continue what you're doing. Then we can explore other ways to use my cock in a bit." The last was said with a growl.

She snorted and shook her head before leaning back to look at him. "We've been mated for a while now, and I never get over the fact that I love touching you so much."

He would have brought her up to him and laid her down on the bed right then, but she wrapped her fist around his dick and sucked on the tip. His eyes rolled to the back of his head as she went down on him, her tongue rolling along his shaft as he went deeper into her mouth. She bobbed her head, her hand rubbing along the places her mouth couldn't reach, all the while licking and sucking until his eyes just about crossed.

Her hand went to his balls, rolling them in her palm, and he had to pull away, afraid he'd blow right then. He might have been a werewolf, and he would have been able to get hard again right away, but he didn't want to come down her throat. No, he wanted to be deep inside her for their first time together alone in so long.

He brought her to his lips, his tongue tangling with hers as their mouths met, their kiss heated. Her nipples were hard little points against his chest, and he growled, *wanting more.*

Wanting it all.

"Hey, I wasn't finished," Willow said on a pant as he trailed his lips along her neck.

He nibbled around where he'd put his mate mark the first time and grinned. Wolves healed quickly, and no one could actually see the mark, but they could tell it was there, almost as if they had a sixth sense.

He might just have to nibble and bite a bit more so that they could remember the mark and the meaning behind it.

Maybe she'd even bite him as well.

His cock twitched against her belly, and he figured biting sounded like a perfect idea.

"I want to come in you, with you. Please." His hands cupped her ass, bringing her even closer to him. He massaged the globes, spreading her just a bit so he could run his fingers between her cheeks.

She gasped as his hands found her puckered hole, and he grinned.

"Lie down on the bed. I'm in charge. Remember?"

She didn't sound as sure as she had when they'd started, but he didn't care. As long as they were together, anything was perfection.

He moved back and lay on the bed, his hands raised so he could help her straddle him. They didn't need a condom since having another baby was always in the back of their minds.

That meant he could feel her around him while he was bare, skin to skin.

Fuck yeah.

Their eyes met, and she took one hand and lowered it so she could guide him in. He swallowed hard as his cock slid into her pussy, one achingly slow inch at a time. Their breath came in pants as she sank onto him until she was fully seated and his cock was deep within her.

"Sweet goddess, you've never felt better, baby."

"I feel like it's been ages. I love you so much, Jasper."

He reached up and framed her face. "I love you too, my mate, my Willow. Now ride me."

She grinned and gave a small nod before moving. Her hips rocked back and forth as she settled on him, both of them remembering how much they loved this. How much they'd missed this. Finally, she moved up slowly, her hands on his shoulders for balance, and they both groaned. She sank back onto him then moved again, riding him slowly, picking up the pace until they were both out of breath.

He reached up and plucked at her nipples then raised his head so he could suck one into his mouth. Her sweet taste danced on his tongue, and he growled, wanting more.

Willow moved up and threw her head back, her breasts bouncing as she rode him. He gripped her hips and moved his own, thrusting into her with all his strength. She looked down and met his gaze, his name a whisper on her lips as the walls of her pussy clamped down on him, her orgasm taking her over. His balls tightened, and that surge of sensation shot down his spine as he came within her, spilling his seed and filling her.

She kept moving her hips, milking him until, finally, she collapsed on top of him, their heartbeats synced together, their wolves howling at their closeness. All Jasper could do was wrap his arms around her and kiss her temple.

"I don't think it's ever been that good," he rasped out.

"We'll just have to practice again to make sure. You know, just in case."

He chuckled, even as his cock hardened within her. "I think I'm up for that."

She rolled her eyes at his not-so-subtle joke but took his lips in a sweet kiss.

"I've missed you," she whispered.

He swallowed hard, tears threatening to fill his eyes. "Me too, Willow. Me too."

CHAPTER FOUR

"Cookie?"

Edward Jamenson paused in the middle of the sentence he'd been trying to read and looked down at his two-year-old granddaughter.

Brie had her tiny fist full of half-eaten cookie, waving it in his direction. He smiled at the one pigtail still up on top of her head. The other one Pat had put in her hair that morning was long gone. Now a little tangle of brown hair seemed to be in its place.

He leaned down and nibbled on the edge of the sugar cookie. She'd left part of it clear from her mouth, so it wasn't as damp as it could have been. With one last look at the texts he should have been reading, he pulled away from his desk and held out his arms.

Brie scrambled onto his lap and stuck her nose in his neck. He hugged her hard, that ache from not having babies this age of his own anymore coming and going quickly. He wasn't as bad as Pat when it came to missing their children as babies, but he had his moments.

He kissed Brie's cheek then moved so they were face to face. She had his eyes. The same eyes of her father. The same eyes of *his* father.

She was a Jamenson through and through, and Edward would not let anything happen to this little girl.

Nor would he let anything happen to any of his other grandchildren who seemed to be growing in number almost daily.

"You're sweeter than the cookie, princess." She put her free hand on his face, and he could hear the stubble from his beard scraping her hand. He held back a curse that he hadn't shaved that morning like he usually did, but he'd been stressed.

Something was coming, something far worse than they'd been through so far, and he didn't know how to fix it.

Hence the reason he was studying the ancient texts the elders had let him borrow. He needed to see if there was a way to take down a demon from hell.

Right now, though, he didn't want to think about any of that. No, he wanted only to deal with the little ball of goodness and light in his arms.

Brie stared at him and tilted her head, a movement so like Jasper it made Edward blink. "You look sad, Grandpa."

She kissed his nose, and his wolf, the strongest in the Redwood Pack and one of the most dominant in the entire country, bowed his head, the love for this little girl ignoring—at least for the moment—any hierarchy and power it held.

"I'm not sad now that you're here." He didn't lie, not then. Brie and her cousins were the ones he was fighting for. He wanted to ensure their futures and would do anything to make that happen.

Jasper and Willow were at the cabin and had been for almost a day now since it was around noon. They would be coming home within the next day to do what they had to within the Pack, but for right then, Edward could feel, within their bonds, that they were at peace.

He'd failed his son. He hadn't been able to see that Jasper needed more help until it was almost too late. He'd almost lost his son because he'd been focused on other things.

There was no excuse for that, and he wouldn't let that happen again.

"You're sad again, Grandpa," Brie said then kissed his cheek. Edward grinned then ate the rest of the cookie in her hand. Her eyes widened, and her mouth opened. "You ate all my cookie!"

He swallowed and grinned. "Yep. Guess you were too slow. Looks like we'll have to get you another."

"With frosting?" Her eyes glittered, and Edward laughed.

"We'll see if that can be arranged."

"Are you stealing cookies from babies now, Alpha?" Pat asked as she strolled into the room.

Edward looked up at his mate and the love of his life and sighed. He loved her just as much today, if not more, than he had when they first set the bond. Her light brown hair framed her face, and she had a dash of flour on her cheek from baking with Brie. He'd always found her softer than the other wolves, rounder in some cases. The physical shell, though, surrounded a woman with a backbone of steel.

Brie turned in Edward's lap so she was facing Pat. "He said he'd get me another one so it's okay, Grandma."

Pat raised a brow then walked over to them, a smile forming on her face. She was just as much of a sucker as he was when it came to their grandchildren—though he might have been worse. He might be Alpha, but he spoiled the kids rotten before he handed them off to their parents on sugar highs.

It was really the only way to treat grandkids.

Pat ran a hand over Brie's head then through his hair. He'd been growing it as long as Jasper's recently, and he knew he needed to cut it. He just hadn't had the motivation to do so. Other things were more important—like the two females in the room with him.

"I suppose we have another cookie for you in the kitchen, darling," Pat said, her eyes on Edward. "The frosting kind, right? Isn't that what the two of you were saying?"

His mate's hearing scared him sometimes.

"I love frosting," Brie said, and Edward just smiled at his mate.

"You heard her. She loves frosting."

"And I bet it doesn't hurt that you happen to love those types of cookies too?"

"Doesn't hurt a bit."

Her eyes skimmed over his shoulder at the texts on his desk, but he gave a small shake of his head. He could take an hour with Brie and Pat and enjoy himself before he went back to his duties.

She nodded then picked Brie off his lap. The three of them had made it into the kitchen when the front door opened to reveal Logan and Caitlin. Edward narrowed his eyes at the new Redwood wolf who seemed to be walking a little too close to his precious, precious daughter.

Cailin caught the look and growled. "Dad."

"What?" he asked, his voice all innocence.

Edward glared at Logan who smiled at Caitlin and then met Edward's gaze without blinking. Oh yes, there would be a long talk about what *exactly* was going on between his only daughter and this wolf.

Soon.

"Cookie!" Brie screamed from beside him, and Cailin smiled brightly at her niece.

"With the frosting? You know, munchkin, those are Grandpa's and my favorites, right?"

"Uh huh. That's why I wanted them. It makes Grandpa happy."

Edward blinked hard, something looking oddly like tears threatening to fill his eyes.

He wouldn't cry at a sweet little girl's words. Not when Logan was so near.

No, he needed to act the strong Alpha and father of the Redwood Pack princess, not like the grandpa who wanted to hug his granddaughter close and forget about the war, if only for a moment.

They munched on cookies and talked about trivial things before finally discussing exactly what Cailin would be doing to help her brother.

"I know I'm not connected like you are, Dad. But I can help."

Edward looked at his daughter, the one who had been trying to navigate her way through the Pack and find her place for so long. She'd been floundering.

"I think you can, Cailin. I trust you."

Cailin's eyes widened, and Pat smiled behind her. He felt Logan's pleasure at the thought of Cailin's happiness, and that settled his own wolf some. Logan would be good for Cailin once they figured out what they wanted.

"I won't let you down."

Brie pulled herself onto Cailin's lap and kissed her cheek. "Of course you won't. You're a Jamenson."

Out of the mouths of babes.

Edward smiled at his family and settled into his chair. The war would rage, and battles would be fought, but if he didn't have the strength in body and mind that came with that came with knowing he had something to fight for, he wouldn't make it.

The Jamensons wouldn't let the Pack down.

He thought back to Jasper and Willow and why they'd needed the break.

It was time to make sure the Pack didn't let the Jamensons down.

CHAPTER FIVE

"Mmm..." Willow hummed to herself, her eyes still closed. Her husband and mate's hands cupped her breasts like he'd done so many times before, but this time, it felt as though it was the first time.

It always felt as if it was the first time with Jasper even when it felt new and different too. He always muddled her brain in the best ways.

She didn't care if she sounded like some dreamy-eyed romantic because, frankly, she was. Sure, the world was crazy and falling apart around them, but she had Jasper. She'd be okay.

Of course she'd fight alongside the rest of them and prove herself as a wolf, but right now, in this little cabin, she and Jasper were all that mattered.

As her mate was currently running his hand down her belly toward the soft hairs on her mound, she put away any thoughts of war and ugliness and focused on him. Honestly, she could barely think straight as it was. She just needed to hone in on that hand of his and those nimble fingers.

"Oh God," she moaned as he flicked his thumb over her clit. She leaned back, craning her neck so she could find his mouth. His tongue met hers as he slid his fingers in and out of her heat, his thumb running circles over that little bundle of nerves. Her nipples hardened against his palm cupping her breast as a wash of hot tingles went over her and she came on his hand, rocking back and forth to let the pleasure last.

"Jasper, gods, I can't take anymore," she whispered, and he growled against her neck.

He moved his hand, making her whimper at the loss, then pulled her thigh up so he could slide between her legs. She loved this position, her back to his front while they lay on their sides. There was something so intimate about it, so special.

"Are you sure, my wolf?"

She arched her back, moving her butt closer to him, wanting him. "Take me, please."

He chuckled against her skin, the rough sensation almost making her come again. "You changed your mind rather quickly."

"Shut up. I'm allowed to want you in the morning, so please, please, just fill me."

"As you wish," he said then bit her shoulder. His fangs slid into her skin, marking her as his mate again, though it felt like the first time. The bond flared between them as their wolves howled. Their breath and heartbeats synced as he marked her once more.

She came again, surprised she could do so soon after the last. Jasper's cock filled her until she felt ready to burst—but in the best possible way. He pumped in and out of her, his hand on her neck, forcing her gaze to his over her shoulder. She moved her hips in tune with his, thrust for thrust.

Their bodies rocked together, their breaths coming in pants.

"Love you," he whispered, and she smiled.

She'd never get tired of those words.

"Love you too."

He thrust again, this time harder than before while his fingers brushed her clit. They came together, their names on each other's lips as his seed filled her.

She'd never get tired of that either.

"That was the best way to wake up in the morning," Jasper said after he'd pulled out and turned her so they were face to face. "Wish we could do it every morning."

She kissed his jaw, the stubble scraping her lips deliciously. "If we did it every morning, it wouldn't be as special."

He raised a brow, and she laughed.

"Fine, it would still be special. I was just trying to make it better since we have Brie trying to walk in on us every morning."

"Is it wrong that I kind of miss that? Well, not that, but I miss our little girl. I know we're here for a break and to breathe, but I want to see her soon."

She smiled, falling in love with her mate all over again. "I wouldn't love you as much as I did if you were any different. Why don't we shower and get dressed? Then I'll make breakfast while you call her. I want to talk to her too."

He nipped at her lips, a soft growl sending pleasure through her body. "As long as we shower together, that sounds like a deal. And I'm not going to ask if you need help cooking this morning because I know that's your thing and you actually like doing it. So weird."

She smacked his ass as they laughed. "Shut it. I'm not weird. I just like baking."

His lips met hers, a soft kiss filled with promise. "I like your baking, so it's a win-win. Now jump in the shower. I want to watch your ass move as you walk."

With a roll of her eyes, she got up and made sure to add an extra wiggle in her step. From the way he growled and then pounced on her, she had a feeling the wiggle helped.

A lot.

Once they were finished showering and recovering from weak knees, she went about making their breakfast. While she was setting up, she called Brie and listened to her little girl gush before she gave the phone to Jasper. Since she'd made omelets the first time she'd cooked for him in his house—which had gone on to become their house—she made them again. Cailin had been amazing and had helped her pack everything she and Jasper would need if they were to stay a week by themselves.

She heard Jasper on the phone with Brie as their daughter talked about her day and all the time they'd missed. It put a little clutch in her heart that she wasn't there with her baby to rock her to sleep, but she knew Brie was in good hands. Willow just had a touch of mommy guilt. She'd already talked to Brie and now Jasper was on round two. There was no doubt that little girl had Willow's big, tough mate wrapped around her finger.

It was freaking adorable.

When he hung up, she was just setting down their plates, the smell of cheese, eggs, and bacon making her mouth water. She loved cooking and didn't care who knew it. Cooking for her mate though?

Priceless.

She could fight alongside him as a wolf and provide for him in ways that he couldn't. That was what mating was about, finding ways to work together and fulfilling each other's needs. She wasn't as strong as he was, but it didn't matter that she didn't possess the fighting skills he'd honed over a century. She'd learn what she needed to and then make sure their family was safe in other ways.

Jasper had his talents.

She had hers.

It was perfect.

Well, it would be once they found a way to balance it all. That was one of the reasons they were there after all.

"Have fun with Brie?" she asked as Jasper walked toward her.

"She's enjoying time with Grandpa and Grandma and is talking a mile a minute. I don't know if my parents realize just what they signed up for."

She smiled and started to soak the pan she'd cooked the omelets in before Jasper gripped her wrist. "I'm just soaking it, Jas."

"Let it stay in the water then. Don't you think about doing the dishes. I'll take care of them after we eat. You cooked. I'll clean. You want to sit on the porch and eat? Get some nature in while we can?"

She raised a brow. "You do realize we live in the middle of a forest and get nature all the time, right?"

"Yes, but this is alone nature. It's different."

She snorted but picked up their coffees and followed him out as he carried their plates. Shuffling a bit, she sat next to him on the bench. The air was crisp and fresh, much like it was at home, but maybe because they were alone, it felt different.

They ate in silence, enjoying their surroundings. Her wolf nudged at her but only to get closer to Jasper's wolf. They'd have to go on a hunt soon, but not today. Today was all about the man and the woman. Their wolves would have their turn.

"See? Nice, right?" Jasper asked as he put down their dishes.

"It's beautiful. I'm glad we both got a chance to come out here."

"Thanks for doing this, Willow. I know I've been hard on you, or at least I feel like I've been."

"What? Of course you haven't been. Why on earth would you think that?"

He turned toward her on the bench, his expression a mixture of stress and guilt. It didn't make any sense to her why he'd look like that, why he'd feel this way.

"I've been putting you and Brie to the side, or at least inadvertently doing so. I feel like I'm lost. I can't do everything I need to do, and I'm not even thinking of things that I *want* to do. I hate this. Did you know that Kade kicked my ass while we were training? He didn't even mean to punch me that hard, but I was too slow to duck. I'm tired, Willow, and I don't know what to do." He ran his hands through his hair, his mouth in a frown.

She'd never heard the defeatist tone coming from him before. She cupped his face and brought his gaze to hers. "Stop it.

Just stop it. We're here because we are going to figure out a way to make things work. You can't put the weight of the world on your shoulders. You need to share the load." He opened his mouth to speak, and she cut him off. "No, listen to me. You are a good Beta. You care for your Pack like they are your own flesh and blood. They can't ask for anything more than that. You also can't do it all."

He inhaled, and she kissed him softly, needing his touch just for the brief moment.

"Jasper, honey, you aren't a failure. You might be tired, but I can see the circles under your eyes fading even as we speak. Just being out here and knowing we have time to work things out for you, us, everyone is helping you. You know it just as I do. Now, as for when we get home? Well, you're not going to be alone there either. Cailin is going to be your new assistant."

He blinked, and then a slow grin spread over his face

"A Beta's assistant? I was thinking I needed something like that, but only in passing."

She kissed his nose then rolled her eyes. "See? This is why we're mates. We totally think along the same lines. Or at least we do when you get a full night's sleep. Now, Cailin can't do it all, but that's why you're there, to tell her what to do." She frowned. "Or at least tell her as much as she'll let you. You know Cailin. She'll want to take charge."

Jasper snorted a laugh—exactly what she'd intended—and relaxed. She leaned against him, and he wrapped an arm around her.

"She's a little obsessive about details," he agreed.

"And exactly what you need. Now what is this about you fighting Kade?"

She felt him move ,and she looked over her shoulder at him running a hand through his hair. "We were training with Logan, and I caught a punch with my face when I should have ducked. I know it was because I was tired, but hell, that's not a good enough excuse. What if I'm not good enough to protect you and Brie? What if I'm so *tired* that I end up getting you or our daughter hurt? What if I'm not good enough?" he repeated.

She moved to sit on his lap and cupped his face, bringing her forehead down to his. "You're stronger than you think you are. Plus, you were fighting with Kade and let your guard down. You're allowed to do that. You don't have your guard down now, do you? No. You're looking around us at this very moment, and I can feel your wolf checking for intruders and anyone near the wards. You are looking for them. You are *always* on guard."

"I have to be."

"Of course. I'm trying to do the same thing. So we can't cut back on that, we can't cut back on our family, and we can't cut back on your duties as Beta. But what we *can* do is let Cailin and others take some of the work. You can learn to delegate. It's okay to do so. It's okay to ask for help."

He let out a shuddering breath. "You undo me with your strength."

"I wouldn't be as strong without you. That's why we work so well together. That's why we're fated."

She kissed him softly then leaned back again, needing time just to be in his arms. They sat there for a while, on watch as always but as relaxed as they'd ever been. She knew they'd have to go back to the den soon, and she honestly couldn't wait to see Brie again, but just then, it was only her and Jasper.

Nothing else mattered.

Her wolf sensed it before she could.

She sat up, her body on edge, though she didn't know why. "Jasper?" she whispered, and he squeezed her arm, his body rock hard behind hers.

Her mate stood and Willow followed, her gaze on the tree line. Their cabin was surrounded by large trees that reached toward the sky and blocked most of their view. She knew the wards were near because she could feel their magic pulsating, but it wasn't a bad kind of tingle. No, it was more like the wards were comforting her, letting her know that they were there to keep the intruders out.

The Centrals, though, with their tainted demonic blood, could slide through the weakest points of the wards if they tried hard enough. Usually it took the demon, Caym, by their side for it to work, but sometimes, a stronger wolf could make it through.

She inhaled, trying to pick up the scent of whatever was putting her on edge. She could scent her mate, the warm and dangerous forest mixed with the smells of man, as well as the small animals around them.

There was something, though, something coming.

"Willow, you should go into the house," Jasper said, his voice low and spoken in that deadly calm that set the hairs on the back of her neck on end.

She raised her brows, though she knew he couldn't see her. "I can have your back." She pulled out her cell phone and had it ready to dial Kade if needed. "I will call Kade if we need backup, but I can't tell what's out there. Plus, I might not be able to fight like you, but I can still fight better than most. Let me help."

Jasper looked over his shoulder quickly and gave her a tight nod. "We've done training with the two of us, but I don't want you hurt, baby," he said when he turned back. "I think there's one wolf out there trying to breach our wards. They aren't through yet, so it's probably a scout looking for weaknesses."

"What's your plan?" Her wolf prowled beneath her skin, ready to fight alongside its mate.

Jasper moved his head slowly, as if surveying the area, and she followed the movement.

There.

A lone wolf stood right at the edge of their wards. She could feel his presence and sense that he was on alert, but hadn't moved toward them. The scent of him was like a sickly sweet taste on her tongue and made her want to gag, but she kept the scent close. The tainted scent was that of a Central wolf.

One that, if her mate had anything to say about it, wouldn't make it back to the Centrals as their scout.

"We'll go out to where he is but come up the side way and upwind so he can't catch our scents. He's not moving toward us, and he doesn't scent as if he is on alert, so I don't think he can tell we're here. We can go through the wards easily, so I want to take him out on the other side. He already smells tainted. His soul is a lost cause."

She nodded, knowing if it had been any other way, he'd have tried to save the wolf. Now, though, they were at war and dying because of the Centrals.

There wasn't time for doubt.

She followed him at a lope, keeping her senses open in case there was another scout in hiding. Jasper slowed, his wolf coming to the surface, brushing hers along the bond.

She could see the other wolf, but it wasn't looking at them. No, the man in ragged jeans and bare chest looked off in the distance but seemed to have no clue they were there.

Good.

With one last look over his shoulder at her, Jasper bounded through the wards. She followed, her claws ready to break through her fingertips if needed. Her mate had the other wolf by the neck before she could blink. Jasper's eyes glowed gold, his wolf close to the surface, ready to shift, but he wasn't breathing hard.

No, Jasper was in full control.

She kept them in the corner of her eye as she checked around them. No other wolves breached her senses, but that didn't mean they couldn't appear quickly. It wouldn't be good to let her guard down.

"What are you doing here?" Jasper growled.

"Watching for you, Redwood filth," the wolf choked out, trying to speak around Jasper's hand, currently squeezing the bastard's windpipe.

"Did you know we were out here?" Jasper asked.

The wolf said nothing.

"Were you sent out here to watch us or just the cabin?"

Again, no answer.

"Are you watching all of our wards looking for weaknesses?"

The wolf blinked as if bored, even though he was clearly in pain.

"Did Caym send you? Are there others with you?"

The wolf didn't say anything and Jasper knew no matter what he did, the wolf wouldn't talk. It was pointless.

Jasper just shook his head then squeezed, breaking the wolf's neck. He dropped the man to the ground and sighed.

"Their scouts have no power, yet they're beating us," he whispered. "Scouts might not need to have power since all they do is watch and report, but they're winning."

She tugged at his hand and pulled him back through the wards, wanting to make sure they were covered.

"Caym is trying to annihilate us all. He won't succeed. He's underestimating us, and we're not going to roll over for him. Remember that."

He kissed her hard then leaned against her slightly but not putting too much of his weight on her. "I just killed a wolf in front of you, and you're not even blinking."

"Jasper, my love, you were so afraid you couldn't protect me, yet what did you just do? You made sure the threat was eliminated before it could escalate. You're a powerful wolf and a wonderful mate. Stop selling yourself short."

"You believe in me more than I deserve sometimes."

She slapped his shoulder and rolled her eyes. "Stop it with the emo, Jasper. You're stronger than you give yourself credit for, and you trusted me enough to be by your side. Now let's call Kade and have him or Adam send someone to clean up. The patrols should be around soon anyway for this sector if I remember, but it never hurts to be sure. I also know that we wanted to stay a bit longer, but now that we had to deal with a Central, I want to just go home to Brie."

Her mate smiled softly then kissed her, a brush of lips that calmed her wolf. "Let's go see our daughter. I don't want to miss another moment. "

Willow wrapped her arms around Jasper's waist and laid her head on his chest. The trip had done what it was meant to do, and he'd found his confidence again. Her wolf nudged at her, and she snuggled closer, tightening her grip. This was her fate, her happiness. She'd fought for it and would fight again, no matter what.

CHAPTER SIX

His mate wiggled up against him in his sleep, and he grinned. Yes, this was a familiar feeling, and Jasper loved every moment of it. His eyes closed, he ran his hand up her shirt to cup her breast. They were under the covers, their bodies tangled and heavy from a long night's sleep, and yet all he wanted to do was claim his mate.

Again.

She arched against him, that little moan escaping her lips such a sweet sound and going straight to his cock.

"Shh, my Willow, don't moan so loud. We wouldn't want to wake anyone."

She laughed softly and turned in his arms. The movement forced him to release her breast, so he moved his hand down to her ass instead.

"Copping a feel this early?" she asked, her voice warm and inviting.

He took her lips, slow and easy, her taste mingling with his, igniting his wolf. "It's never too early to cop a feel."

They both burst out in laughter, their bodies shaking together. "Oh my god, that's got to be the worst line you've ever used on me."

He frowned. "I'm sure I've used worse. I'll strive to do better with bringing you horrible pick-up lines."

"Oh Jeez. What have we started?" She smiled while her eyes danced.

"Well, I know what *I* started, and it included getting you out of these shorts and having a breakfast of my own before we get out of bed."

Her eyes darkened. "Don't let me be the one to stop you."

"Mommy! Daddy!" The sound of a little fist knocking on the door made both of them freeze.

"Well, at least she's knocking now," Willow said deadpan, and Jasper chuckled.

"There's always that, I guess." He moved off his mate and ran a hand through his hair. "Come in, Brie."

The door opened, and he saw the top of her head at the end of the bed as she padded in quickly. He reached down when she moved to the side of the bed and then pulled her to sit between him and Willow. She blinked up at him and squirmed, her body radiating more energy than usual.

"Good morning, baby girl. What's got you all fiery today?"

His wolf rubbed up against his skin, and he held back a strained smile. He had a feeling he knew exactly what was going on with Brie, but he wanted to see what she thought of it first.

She scrunched up her face and rubbed her arms. "I don't know. It's like my skin is itchy, but I don't know why." Her eyes filled with tears, and her lower lip wobbled. "What's wrong with me, Daddy?"

Sweet Jesus, he wanted to crawl in a hole and die or at least find a way to make everything in the world right again. While the change was brutal and painful with adults, the moon goddess was kind to children. Their shift would be painless and feel like a hug. It wouldn't be until they hit puberty that it would really hurt.

Thankfully.

Most thought that the moon goddess spared the children from the pain but then couldn't stop it from happening after a certain point. After all, the idea of becoming a werewolf had been a punishment for hunting long ago. Changing one's shape into something completely different *should* hurt. It wasn't magic and rainbows, but a body transforming cell by cell.

He hugged her close, and Willow leaned into them both. He wrapped an arm around his girls and tried to be strong in accepting the realization that his little girl was growing up.

"It's your wolf, Brie. You're almost ready to shift so your skin feels all itchy because your wolf wants to come out."

She blinked then smiled wide, her tears gone in a flash. "I get to be a wolf like Finn!"

He snorted. "I take it you're not scared."

"Nuh huh. I get to be a wolf like you and Mommy and Finn." She scrambled off the bed and tugged at him. "Come on. Let's go. Wolfie time!" She ran off at top speed, screaming and giggling.

"You heard her. It's wolfie time," Willow said, the false cheer in her voice not hiding her worry from him.

"She'll be okay, Willow."

"You sure it doesn't hurt for babies?"

They both stood by the bed, and he kissed her softly. "I'm sure. She'll love it. When she gets to be a little older, then we'll deal with the shifts that hurt. Right now, we get to watch our daughter find her wolf."

Willow let out a breath and tugged on her jeans. "Well, come on then. Brie's probably in the middle of our backyard naked as a jaybird." She paused. "Will we have to shift with her?"

Jasper shook his head. "Maybe. She might be able to get it on her own since she's seen us shift before. If she needs us though, either one of us can.

His mate snorted then strode toward the backyard where they indeed found a naked Brie running round making howling sounds.

"Why can't I be a wolf now?" she asked, her eyes wide.

"Because you need to focus, baby girl." Jasper went to the middle of the yard and sat cross-legged. "Kneel like a wolf and then focus on the part that itches under your skin. Do you want Mommy to show you how to shift?"

She shook her head, her teeth biting into her lower lip as she concentrated. "I've seen it before. I can do it."

There was something so confident in her tone that Jasper had to blink. Brie seemed to be full of surprises. Gods, she was going to be a handful when she became a teenager.

He shook his head so he could focus on Brie's shift. Willow sat on the other side of her, and they both rubbed up and down Brie's back. His wolf felt the stirrings of her little wolf, and he smiled.

Any minute now.

"Close your eyes and try to find that little ball of energy."

"Okay," she said, her voice determined.

"Now tug on that a bit. Think of it like tug of war and you're trying to win against Finn."

"I can beat him. He's a boy, but I'm tough too."

"Yes, you are honey. Now feel that energy and pull."

She nodded then gasped, as she found it. Jasper's wolf howled, and he felt Willow's do the same through the bond. Fur sprouted under his palm, and where once a little girl knelt, now stood a tiny pure white wolf pup with green eyes.

"Oh, baby, you're so adorable. You did it!" Tears streamed down Willow's face, and he had a feeling he was crying too.

Brie wiggled from between them and took a couple shaky steps before turning back and jumping on Willow. Willow laughed as Brie licked her face, and then Brie moved to do the same to Jasper.

Right then and there, he fell in love with his daughter all over again.

She had to be the cutest wolf in the history of wolf pups. She wagged her little tail then pranced away, dancing as much as a wolf could, and Jasper just shook his head.

"She's so good at that," Willow said, awe in her voice.

He stood, pulling his mate up with him, then wrapped an arm around her. "She was meant for it. She's meant for so much."

Willow laid her head on his chest, and he tightened his hold. "We're going to make sure she gets to do just that, find out what she's meant for, and also have a chance to one day watch her own little pup run and play. We're going to do that for her, Jasper."

He blinked away the tears and turned to face her. He cupped her face and nodded. "We're going to win, Willow. We have more to fight for, and we won't give up. That little girl is going to be happy, happier than she is now if that's possible. You know why I know that?"

"Why?"

"Because I have you by my side. You're my haven, my everything, Willow. You're the one who will do whatever it takes to fight for what you love, and I can only do what I can to keep up. We're going to win because we have each other and have a future worth fighting for."

"I love you, Jasper."

"I love you too, Willow, my haven."

They turned and watched their little wolf pup dance in the

grass, and right then, Jasper knew that, no matter what happened, this moment, this scene, would be something he'd never forget. He had everything he needed, and now that he had a plan, he knew exactly how he was going to keep it that way.

As long as he had Willow by his side, he could do anything.

Coming Next in the Redwood Pack world:

The Redwood Pack Princess and the wolf that just might save them all get their story in the final installment of the Redwood Pack: Fighting Fate, coming June 2014

A Note from Carrie Ann

Thank you so much for reading **A BETA'S HAVEN**. It was so nice to go back and visit Jasper and Willow after all this time. Things sure have changed in the Redwood Pack! I do hope if you liked this story, that you would please leave a review. Not only does a review spread the word to other readers, they let us authors know if you'd like to see more stories like this from us. I love hearing from readers and talking to them when I can. If you want to make sure you know what's coming next from me, you can sign up for my newsletter at www.CarrieAnnRyan.com; follow me on twitter at @CarrieAnnRyan, or like my Facebook page. I also have a

Facebook Fan Club where we have trivia, chats, and other goodies. You guys are the reason I get to do what I do and I thank you.

Make sure you're signed up for my MAILING LIST so you can know when the next releases are available as well as find giveaways and FREE READS.

I love going back and visiting characters. Adam and Bay were the hardest couple to write out of the entire Redwood Pack. They crushed me in their need for each other and the obstacles they had to overcome to find their future. This novella was a way to show you what happened once they were a mated couple in truth. Throughout the Redwood Pack series, you will be able to read more after the HEA novellas, so keep an eye out!

I'm also not leaving this world completely. You've met

some of the Talons and because I fell for Gideon the first time he walked on the page to help the Redwoods, I knew I had to tell his story. I also knew I wanted to write some of the Redwood Pack children's stories. Rather than write two full series where I wasn't sure how they would work together, I'm doing one better. The Talon Pack series will be out in early 2015. It is set thirty years in the future and will revolve around the Talon Pack and how they are interacting in the world and with the Redwoods. Because it's set thirty years in the future, I get to write about a few of the Redwood Pack children finding their mates.

The first novel will be about the Talon Alpha Gideon and....Brie, Jasper and Willow's daughter thirty years from now.

Redwood Pack Series:
Book 1: An Alpha's Path
Book 2: A Taste for a Mate
Book 3: Trinity Bound
Book 3.5: A Night Away
Book 4: Enforcer's Redemption
Book 4.5: Blurred Expectations
Book 4.7: Forgiveness
Book 5: Shattered Emotions
Book 6: Hidden Destiny
Book 6.5: A Beta's Haven
Book 7: Fighting Fate
Book 7.5 Loving the Omega
Book 7.7: The Hunted Heart
Book 8: Wicked Wolf

Want to keep up to date with the
next Carrie Ann Ryan Release?
Receive Text Alerts easily!
Text CARRIE to 24587

About Carrie Ann and her Books

New York Times and USA Today Bestselling Author Carrie Ann Ryan never thought she'd be a writer. Not really. No, she loved math and science and even went on to graduate school in chemistry. Yes, she read as a kid and devoured teen fiction and Harry Potter, but it wasn't until someone handed her a romance book in her late teens that she realized that there was something out there just for her. When another author suggested she use the voices in her head for good and not evil, The Redwood Pack and all her other stories were born.

Carrie Ann is a bestselling author of over twenty novels and novellas and has so much more on her mind (and on her spreadsheets *grins*) that she isn't planning on giving up her dream anytime soon.

www.CarrieAnnRyan.com

Redwood Pack Series:
Book 1: An Alpha's Path
Book 2: A Taste for a Mate
Book 3: Trinity Bound
Book 3.5: A Night Away
Book 4: Enforcer's Redemption
Book 4.5: Blurred Expectations
Book 4.7: Forgiveness
Book 5: Shattered Emotions
Book 6: Hidden Destiny
Book 6.5: A Beta's Haven
Book 7: Fighting Fate
Book 7.5 Loving the Omega
Book 7.7: The Hunted Heart
Book 8: Wicked Wolf

The Talon Pack (Following the Redwood Pack Series):
Book 1: Tattered Loyalties
Book 2: An Alpha's Choice
Book 3: Mated in Mist (Coming in 2016)

The Redwood Pack Volumes:
Redwood Pack Vol 1
Redwood Pack Vol 2
Redwood Pack Vol 3
Redwood Pack Vol 4
Redwood Pack Vol 5
Redwood Pack Vol 6

Montgomery Ink:
Book 0.5: Ink Inspired
Book 0.6: Ink Reunited
Book 1: Delicate Ink
Book 1.5 Forever Ink
Book 2: Tempting Boundaries
Book 3: Harder than Words
Book 4: Written in Ink

The Branded Pack Series: (Written with Alexandra Ivy)
Books 1 & 2: Stolen and Forgiven
Books 3 & 4: Abandoned and Unseen

Dante's Circle Series:
Book 1: Dust of My Wings
Book 2: Her Warriors' Three Wishes
Book 3: An Unlucky Moon
The Dante's Circle Box Set (Contains Books 1-3)
Book 3.5: His Choice
Book 4: Tangled Innocence
Book 5: Fierce Enchantment
Book 6: An Immortal's Song (Coming in 2016)

Holiday, Montana Series:
Book 1: Charmed Spirits
Book 2: Santa's Executive
Book 3: Finding Abigail
The Holiday Montana Box Set (Contains Books 1-3)
Book 4: Her Lucky Love

Book 5: Dreams of Ivory

Tempting Signs Series:
Finally Found You

Excerpt: Loving the Omega

From the next novella in New York Times Bestselling Author Carrie Ann Ryan's Redwood Pack Series

The quick, lethal slice of the blade robbed him of breath, and he gasped, clinging to that last thread of life he knew would fade away as he exhaled. Fire scorched down his throat, down his spine. The absence of pain, the absence of agony was a torture in itself. He reached out, begging, screaming until his voice was raw.

It wouldn't matter though.

It never did.

The darkness surrounded him, clawing, digging its talons

into his skin until he bled dry. It was the same thing every time. No matter what he did, he wouldn't save him. He'd watch him die and lose the connection to the one man who mattered.

He pushed off the enemy and the cloying scent that meant the nothingness had found him and ran through clay and mud to the man who'd fallen, the man who'd been his everything as a child.

"Dad!"

His screams did nothing.

The man fell to the ground, his body burning, turning to ash. There would be no rebirth. No phoenix rising. Only death.

"Maddox! Let go!"

He turned at the sound of his mother's voice, the pain underlying her terror unbearable. She stood in a ring of fire, a sad smile on her face.

"Let go, baby. Stop fighting."

Maddox Jamenson jolted from sleep, a scream on his lips. Sweat slicked his back, and his hands shook. He let his face rest in his hands as he tried to throw off the nightmare as he'd done every morning since his parents had died, but it wasn't enough this time.

He staggered from bed, his feet sliding on the tile when he got to the bathroom, his body still in a state of shock and sleep. As he vacated his stomach of whatever was left over from the night before, he closed his eyes, trying to will away the shakes.

Soft hands rubbed the scars on his back, soothed his aches. His mate, his love, Ellie placed a cool washcloth on his forehead, and he leaned into her, his eyes closed. He knew she sat on the floor next to him, her back to the sink as she took the brunt of his weight. She'd carry him through

fire. Had literally done that once
before. Just as he had done for
her.

Those days were over now. At
least they should have been.

Ellie shifted so he sat
between her legs, supported
against her chest, and ran her
hands through his hair. "Feel
better?"

They'd lain the opposite of
this before, his large body
cradling hers. The picture they
made now would have looked odd
to outsiders, but this was him and
Ellie. They were who they were.
Nothing more. Nothing less.

Maddox nodded, finally
opening his eyes to see his mate.
Her dark hair framed her face,
the worry in her dark eyes mixed
with sleep—sleep they both
should still be relishing in.

"I've been better," he replied
truthfully. He ran his tongue over

his teeth and winced. "And I need to brush my teeth."

Ellie wrinkled her nose then kissed his temple. "Yeah, brushing your teeth sounds good. But what about the nightmare? Was it the same one?"

He sighed, closing his eyes for a moment, before forcing them back open. He was man enough to admit he was too afraid to keep them closed for too long afraid of what he'd see.

"It's the same thing each time. I feel the bond between my father and me snap, sever, break. It's not just the Alpha bond, but the one that holds us together as a family..."

"...and your connection to him as an Omega," his mate finished for him.

Maddox leaned into Ellie's hold once more then stood up, holding out his hand. She put her hand in his, and he pulled her up, tucking her into his body. With her there, his wolf calmed, and he didn't feel so out of place, out of sync anymore. He slid his fingers through her long black hair, loving the soft texture against his skin. Memories of her hair brushing his sweat-slick skin as they made love filled his mind, and he held back a groan. Yes, he loved her hair. The dark tresses fell over her honey-dark skin, the combination a perfect blend of what he loved about his mate.

"Want to talk about it?" she asked through their mental connection.

Their mating bond was unique in that it had held this special feature. They could communicate thoughts to one another along a special path created when they mated. He could hear the thoughts she sent him and vice versa. They couldn't hear every thought, and he was glad for that. Without that barrier it would be easy to become lost inside her mind forever, painful memories and all. If he could, he would find a way to erase everything she'd been through with the Centrals and soothe her aches, but as Ellie had pointed out, without those, she wouldn't be the person she was today. It was the same for him as well. They each needed their own space, but knowing that the other person would be there, even in that special connection, made Maddox feel more centered.

He wasn't sure how the extra power through their mating bond had happened, or if there were true instances beyond rumors of it happening to others, but he was grateful for it.

Before they mated, Maddox had felt that special spark with his Ellie but had also felt cut off from her in a way that terrified him. Not only had he been an idiot in thinking she was his twin brother, *North's*, mate, but he hadn't been able to feel her emotions.

As the Omega, he had that bond with each and every packmember—except his twin. He could feel the highs and lows that came with living, and it was his job to keep the emotional health of the Redwood Pack in alignment.

Without the mating bond, however, he hadn't been able to feel Ellie. That alone had made him feel adrift in an endless stream of pain and loss.

Now, though, he had everything.

Or at least he tried to believe he did.

"No, I don't need to talk about it again," Maddox finally answered. Ellie let out a breath then leaned into him, brushing her teeth at the same time as he did.

They'd discussed his dreams and what they meant over and over in the past month since the Redwoods had defeated Caym and the Centrals, but they couldn't find a way to make them stop.

There was no Omega for the Omega.

Not even the mate who loved him with everything she had could be his Omega.

"Mom? Dad?"

Maddox grinned despite the sour way they'd woken up and pulled Ellie into the bedroom at the sound of their daughter's voice.

"We're in here, Charlotte," he called out, grateful he and Ellie had worn clothes to bed that evening.

Charlotte huffed and rolled her pretty brown eyes—so much

like Ellie's— as she walked into the bedroom. Seven years old and the little girl already had the attitude of a pre-teen.

Not that Maddox cared a bit. Considering how they'd found her, he'd take the attitude and eye-rolling over the abject terror and fear he'd seen the first time they met any day.

"I know you're in here. That's why I knocked first." She said it with a smile and that hint of giddiness that told Maddox she was just happy she could speak whenever she wished.

When they'd first found Charlotte, she'd been chained to a wall in Corbin's basement. Charlotte, fearful and in danger, tried her best to help Maddox and Ellie out of a dangerous situation. As soon as they'd gotten near the girl, they knew who she was.

Hector's daughter.

Corbin's sister.

Ellie's sister.

It hadn't been a hard decision to take Charlotte away from the Centrals and bring her to the Redwoods. In fact, he wasn't sure he and Ellie had talked about it beyond the plan to save the little girl. Once Charlotte became a Redwood, there had been the issue of just *how* to raise her. Others might have raised her as a younger sibling and found a way to deal, but Charlotte desperately needed a mother and father.

The little girl had told them that in plain words.

There was no way to say no to that, and they adopted her as their own.

The fact she called them Mom and Dad, though, that was new. And still a kick in the chest every time he heard it. The good kind of kick, though. The really freaking good kind.

"Can we have French toast?"

Maddox blinked at Charlotte's question then shook his head, trying to clear the cobwebs. His mind had been on the past and what they'd overcome more often than not lately, and he needed to start focusing on the future.

"No? We can't have French toast?" Charlotte asked, her lip wobbling.

Maddox knelt down before picking her up and tossing her over his shoulder. She squealed and wiggled, but he had a firm hold on her. He'd never let his daughter get hurt. No matter what.

"Yes, I'll make you some French toast."

"Do you want me to make it?" Ellie asked behind them, laughter in her voice.

"No," he and Charlotte said at the same time then froze. Maddox turned and pulled

Charlotte so he held her in front of his chest. "Uh..."

Ellie raised a brow and folded her arms over her chest. "You both are way too much alike. And I only burned the French toast once."

Maddox grimaced, remembering the taste. He wouldn't let her throw it out. No, he had to eat it all to prove to her that he was a good mate.

Or a crazy one.

"Ellie, baby..."

His mate winked then tickled Charlotte, who in turn thrashed and ducked in his arms. Soon he was laughing with the both of them, the perfect morning after another shitty night of dreams.

"Crap! Why can't I get this right?"

Maddox winced at Ellie's words but didn't get up from his

spot on the floor. He kept painting Charlotte's dresser as a surprise for her when she got home from the play date in the center of the den.

Ellie had tried baking.

Again.

And from the burnt smell filling his nostrils and the frustration radiating off his mate mixing with the paint fumes, she wasn't doing well. The woman could cook and not kill them. They all knew that. She could make pastas, rice, some sauces, and even dressings.

As soon as she had to add sugar to something and call it a baked good or even French toast, it was like she forgot how to use an oven.

For some reason he thought that was the cutest thing ever. Not that he'd ever tell her that.

"I see that smirk, Maddox Jamenson."

Maddox schooled his features as Ellie came to his side before sitting down. "I have no idea what you're talking about."

Ellie snorted then leaned into him. He set his paintbrush down and wrapped his arm around her shoulders.

"What's up, mate of mine?"

"I will never be able to bake cookies and other things for our girl like Willow does." Willow was Maddox's brother Jasper's mate. She was also an amazing baker and now a chocolatier.

"Baby, that's Willow's job and passion. You don't have to bake as well as her. In fact, you can use her skills to your advantage. We can have cookies without the cleanup."

She sighed then bit into his shoulder softly. His wolf perked up, the slight sting of her teeth against Maddox more than enough to entice him.

"I want to be able to bake *with* Charlotte," Ellie whispered.

Maddox kissed her temple then brought her to his lap. She curled into him, and he ran his hands down her side. He knew this was about more than just baking, but he would wait until she was ready to talk about it. After all, she'd given him time that morning.

"You can. Maybe Charlotte will be a savant at it."

Ellie snorted then leaned into his neck, sniffing before licking behind his ear. It was a slow move, as if she hadn't thought about doing it and just did it instinctively.

Maddox groaned then stood up with her in his arms. Thank the moon goddess he was a wolf with extra strength because getting up from a seated position on the floor with his mate in his arms wouldn't have been easy otherwise. Not that Ellie was heavy by any means, but it could have been awkward as hell.

"Where are we going?" she asked softly.

"I'm going to take you to the bedroom and make love to you and make sure my scent is all over your body."

Ellie licked the underside of his ear again before nipping on the lobe. He growled, the sting of her bite going straight to his cock.

"I'm pretty sure your scent is so deep in my pores there's no way it would ever leave."

Maddox grinned then set her down on the edge of the bed. "I just want to be thorough."

"You look like a wolf on the prowl, you know."

Maddox licked his lips then nipped at hers. "I am, Ellie mine. Now let me strip you down and lick those pretty breasts."

She blushed then lifted her arms, making it easy for him to take off her shirt. When they'd first mated, he'd been soft, gentle, oh-so-sweet. It was what they'd both needed. The pain in Ellie's past, and the strain on his wolf from knowing that past, had forced him to treat her as gently as possible. Not that she was fragile, oh no, she was the furthest from fragile as a mate could be.

She was strong to the core.

And as they became mates in truth and time had passed, they'd explored each other in a heady way. Each time they came together was more explosive than the last, their wolves arching, bonding, and mating in all ways possible.

He took off his clothes as well, leaving both sets in a pile on the floor near the bed. His gaze went to hers, the gold rim around the honey brown glowing in need, in heat. He loved those eyes, loved falling in love with them each time he set eyes on her.

"Love me, Maddox."

Licking his lips, he knelt before her, putting his hands on her knees. "Let me taste you, Ellie mine. You know I love it when you come on my tongue, all sweet and delicious. Like my own taste of candy and nectar."

"You know, I'm starting to crave your dirty talk."

He grinned then spread her legs. As she shuddered under his gaze, he blew cool breath over his pussy, loving the way she tensed then fell back fully on the bed.

"Up on your elbows, Ellie mine. I want to look in your eyes as I lick your pussy."

She shivered, and his wolf growled, wanting more.

Craving more.

He licked her then, the sweet taste bursting on his tongue. She bucked, and he put his arm over her hips, holding her in place so he could lick his way around her, a sweet torture for the both of them. He suckled and licked around her clit, pulling back the hood so he could flick her clit with the tip of his tongue.

She cried out for him, and he hummed against her hood and clit before spearing her with his fingers. He curved them, finding that swollen spot deep within her. He rubbed circles over it as he licked and nibbled her clit. He knew she was close, her body zinging with that special energy that shot right to his cock.

He pressed harder on that bundle of nerves at the same time he bit down on her clit with one fang, a gentle scrape that was more of a dominance play than anything else. They both loved it, and from the way she screamed his name, her gaze never shuttering as those honey brown eyes met his, he knew that he would have to do that move again.

Next time.

Because right then all he wanted was to be deep within her.

He pulled out of her and licked his fingers. A slow movement that had his mate swallowing hard, still gasping for breath from her orgasm.

"I want you on top, Ellie mine," he said as he plucked her off the bed and set her on her feet. "Ride me so I'm deep within that tight pussy of yours."

"You like it when I'm in control, do you?" She grinned then pushed his shoulders so he fell back to the bed, his cock bouncing off his belly.

"You know I love it when you do that hip-roll thing. Sexy as hell."

She straddled him, her hands planted near his head and her slick heat brushing against his dick. "I like it too. I like when you play with my breasts when I ride you. It makes me feel like I'm in control even as you press up deep within me, never letting go."

He almost came right then at the visual. With a grunt, he lifted her up by her hips then slammed her down on his cock. They both groaned, lying still and adjusting to the feeling of her pussy wrapped so delicately around his dick.

She sighed then rolled her hips in that way that made his balls tighten. Fuck, he loved it when she did that.

He cupped her breasts, flicking her nipples. Goddess, he loved her breasts too. Honestly, he loved every single thing about this woman. She lifted up, sliding up his cock, leaving a glistening trail, then slid back down. He groaned but kept his attention on her breasts, knowing that's what she loved. He let her set the pace, because as soon as she came again, it would be his turn.

"Rub yourself against the base of my dick, Ellie," he grunted through the pleasure. "Make yourself come."

She grinned at him then shifted forward so her breasts were near his mouth. He loved the taste of them, he licked and suckled until they were like dark red berries, ready for plucking.

Ellie rolled her hips again, this time grinding her clit against the base of his cock at an agonizing pace. Her breath quickened, her moves becoming frantic as she reached her climax, her pussy clamping down on his dick.

He pulled out in one quick move, flipped her on her back, and then plunged into her before she could come down from her high. She arched her back, her eyes closed.

Goddess, he'd never seen such a beautiful sight.

He gripped her hips, ramming into her with all his strength. They both needed the strength, the pace that sent them over the edge. His balls tightened, the tingling at the base of his back telling him he was close.

"Ellie, open your eyes."

She met his gaze, and he slammed into her once more, staying there as he came within her, filling her up until he was sure she'd always be part of him as he was of her.

Soon after, he lay down beside her, spent yet energized.

He knew they would have to get up soon and get dressed again so they were ready when Charlotte came home, but right then, he was perfectly content with his mate naked in his arms. Things weren't perfect in their den, in their home, but they were well on their way to becoming exactly who they needed to be.

However, it didn't shake the sense of something about to change. Something even his Omega powers couldn't predict.

Dust of My Wings

From New York Times Bestselling Author Carrie Ann Ryan's Dante's Circle Series

Humans aren't as alone as they choose to believe. Every human possesses a trait of supernatural that lays dormant within their genetic make-up. Centuries of diluting and breeding have allowed humans to think they are alone and untouched by magic. But what happens when something changes?

Neat freak lab tech, Lily Banner lives her life as any ordinary human. She's dedicated to her work and loves to hang out with her friends at Dante's Circle, their local bar. When she discovers a strange blue dust at work she meets a handsome stranger holding secrets – and maybe her heart. But after a close call with a thunderstorm, she may not be as ordinary as she thinks.

Shade Griffin is a warrior angel sent to Earth to protect the supernaturals' secrets. One problem, he can't stop leaving dust in odd places around town. Now he has to find every ounce of his dust and keep the presence of the supernatural a secret. But after a close encounter with a sexy lab tech and a lightning quick connection, his millennia old loyalties may shift and he could lose more than just his wings in the chaos.

Warning: Contains a sexy angel with a choice to make and a green-eyed lab tech who dreams of a dark-winged stranger. Oh yeah, and a shocking spark that's sure to leave them begging for more.

Ink Inspired

From New York Times Bestselling Author Carrie Ann Ryan's Montgomery Ink Series

Shepard Montgomery loves the feel of a needle in his hands, the ink that he lays on another, and the thrill he gets when his art is finished, appreciated, and loved. At least that's the way it used to be. Now he's struggling to figure out why he's a tattoo artist at all as he wades through the college frat boys and tourists who just want a thrill, not a permanent reminder of their trip. Once he sees the Ice Princess walk through Midnight Ink's doors though, he knows he might just have found the inspiration he needs.

Shea Little has spent her life listening to her family's desires. She went to the best schools, participated in the most proper of social events, and almost married the man her family wanted for her. When she ran from that and found a job she actually likes, she thought she'd rebelled enough. Now though, she wants one more thing—only Shepard stands in the way. She'll not only have to let him learn more about her in order to get inked, but find out what it means to be truly free.

Printed in Great Britain
by Amazon